*Lucky Star that shines so bright,
Who will need your help tonight?
Light up the sky, it's thanks to you
Wishes really do come true . . .*

Lucky Stars

Explore the sparkling world of the stars at

www.luckystarsbooks.co.uk

Wishes really do come true

Lucky Stars

The Swimming Gala Wish

Phoebe Bright

Illustrated by Karen Donnelly

MACMILLAN CHILDREN'S BOOKS

A Working Partners book

Special thanks to Valerie Wilding

First published 2013 by Macmillan Children's Books
a division of Macmillan Publishers Limited
20 New Wharf Road, London N1 9RR
Basingstoke and Oxford
Associated companies throughout the world
www.panmacmillan.com

ISBN 978-1-4472-3658-0

1 3 5 7 9 8 6 4 2

A CIP catalogue record for this book is available from
the British Library.

Printed and bound by CPI Group (UK) Ltd, Croydon CR0 4YY

To Sean, Tom and Katy,
who make all my good pens disappear!
(KD)

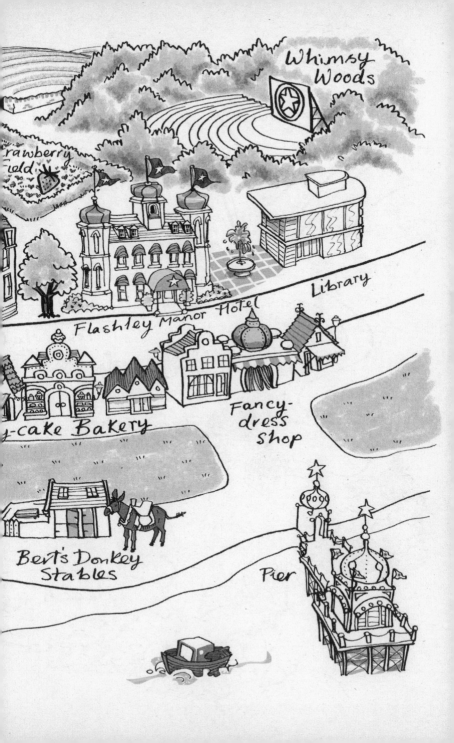

Contents

Contents

Hello, friend!

I'm Stella Starkeeper and I want to tell you a secret. Have you ever gazed up at the stars and thought how magical they looked? Well, you're right. Stars really do have magic!

Their precious glittering light allows me to fly down from the sky, all the way to Earth. You see, I'm always on the lookout for boys and girls who are especially kind and helpful. I train them to become Lucky Stars – people who can make wishes come true!

So the next time you're under the twinkling night sky, look out for me. I'll be floating among the stars somewhere. Do give me a wave!

Love from
Stella x

1
In the Starry Sky

Cassie's dear old cat rubbed his face against hers.

'Stop it, Twinkle!' she murmured. 'It's too early.'

'Miaowwwwwww!' Twinkle patted her with his soft paw.

'What are you trying to tell me?' asked Cassie, sitting up. 'Oh, if only I still had my crescent-moon charm, I could understand you.'

Twinkle nuzzled her hand. 'Miaoww!'

'We'll be able to talk to each other again,' Cassie said, 'as soon as I find my magical charm bracelet.'

She missed so many of her bracelet's powers – the cupcake charm that made her invisible, the butterfly that stopped time,

the heart that gave her perfect memory and the flower that made things appear.

Cassie remembered her seventh birthday, when her magical friend Stella Starkeeper had given her the bracelet. It held one charm then, the little bird that gave her the power to fly. She'd earned more charms by helping to make people's wishes come true. When Cassie received her seventh charm, she became a real Lucky Star, which meant she could actually grant wishes.

But now her beautiful bracelet was gone. Lost? Stolen? All she knew was it

had disappeared two days ago while she
was at the beach with her best friend, Alex,
practising for today's swimming gala.

I should never have left it in my bag, she
thought miserably. But if she'd worn it
while swimming it might have slipped off
her wrist and been lost in the sea forever.

The most awful thing was that losing
the bracelet had caused Stella Starkeeper's
magic to fade. That meant Stella herself was
growing weaker.

Cassie took a silver star from her bedside
table. It was the only charm left. She and
Alex had found it half buried in the sand
when they were searching frantically for
the bracelet. It was her final charm, the one
she'd got when she became a Lucky Star.

With this charm, she could still fly to the Starry Sky – and it also had an extra power, the power to take her to other Lucky Stars, just like herself.

Stella said that if I shared magic with two more Lucky Stars, together we could find my missing bracelet, Cassie thought. She had already found two Lucky Stars, Hannah and Yasmin, and hopefully today she'd get her bracelet back! In fact, this morning she was due to meet Hannah and Yasmin up in the Starry Sky, at the little pink star where she often met Stella.

'Miaoww!'

'Oh, Twinkle,' Cassie said, rubbing the sleep out of her eyes. 'What are you saying?'

9

She gazed up through the glass panel of her domed bedroom ceiling, and gasped. Here and there, a sparkle flashed in the early morning sunshine.

'That's why Twinkle woke me,' Cassie whispered. 'Those sparkles look magical! Maybe they're a sign from Stella.'

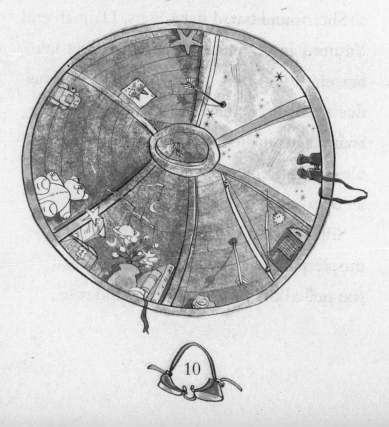

With a *whizz* and a *zip* and a swirling *fizz*, the sparkles whooshed around the dome.

'Wow! It *is* a sign,' Cassie breathed. 'Stella must want to see me. Oh, Twinkle, I hope nothing bad has happened, especially now her powers are fading so fast.'

She concentrated hard on her star charm. A stream of sparkles flowed from it and swirled around Cassie. She tingled all over.

Still wearing her purple star pyjamas, she pulled the lever to open it and rose

Lucky Stars

up through the glass panel in the dome.
Soon she was looking down on her home,
Starwatcher Towers. The big observatory
where her father studied stars and planets
through telescopes was dark. Mum and Dad
were still asleep.

Cassie flew up until the whole town
of Astral-on-Sea lay spread out below. A
single car drove along the high street, but
the beach and pier were deserted. *It'll be
crowded later on for the swimming gala*, she
thought. Cassie rose higher and higher until
she was among the colourful stars bobbing
and dancing around the Starry Sky.

Ahead was the little pink star. Cassie
stared in dismay. Stella was there, but
all Cassie could see was her faint, silvery

outline. Stella's star-tipped wand and silver crown had faded completely, and the tips of her silver boots had disappeared. Even her clothes had lost their shine.

'Stella!' Cassie cried. *I must find my bracelet and save her*, she thought as she flew to the pink star.

Stella's pale face looked sad, but it lit up when she saw Cassie.

They hugged. Cassie felt as if she was holding the softest cloud in her arms.

'I'm glad I had enough magic left to send you a few sparkles,' said Stella. 'I called to you because if you don't find your bracelet today I may have disappeared by the time the evening star shines.'

'You told me to find more Lucky Stars to help me,' said Cassie, 'and I have!'

Before Stella could reply, they heard two shouts.

'Hello!'

'Hi!'

Cassie turned. Flying towards her was a girl with long red hair wearing a dressing gown and wellies, and another with a shiny black ponytail in a tracksuit and trainers.

'Hannah! Yasmin!' cried Cassie. 'Stella, these are the Lucky Stars I found, and

they've promised to share their magic to help find my bracelet. Then your powers will return. Everything will be all right!'

2
The Gala Begins

Stella smiled weakly at Hannah and Yasmin.
'I've heard of you both,' she said.

'Don't you train all the Lucky Stars?'
asked Cassie.

'No, there are other Starkeepers,' said
Stella. 'And your friends have different
charms on their bracelets, with different
powers.'

Yasmin took Stella's pale hand. 'Cassie
made wishes come true for me and Hannah.

We'll share our magic powers and find her bracelet.'

'Let's start searching for it right now,' Cassie said.

'But, Cassie,' said Stella, 'don't you want to race in today's swimming gala?'

'Saving you is much more important than that!' Cassie protested.

Stella looked serious. 'Do you remember that when you were training to be a Lucky Star I gave a clue to help you earn each charm?'

Cassie nodded.

'Well, I can't help you find your bracelet,' Stella continued, sounding tired. 'All I can do is give you a clue. You *must* swim in the gala. It's absolutely vital.'

Cassie was puzzled, but she knew that Stella's clues were always very important. 'Then I will,' she said. 'Hannah, Yasmin, can you come to the swimming gala later?'

'Yes,' said Hannah. 'We'll ask our parents if we can watch your race.' She yawned. 'I got up early to milk our cows. I know we can't use our charms to help ourselves, but I'd love to use my rewind charm to roll back time so I can have a sleep!'

'You can this time,' said Stella, 'as you're helping Cassie.'

'Great!' said Hannah. 'Back to Jupiter

21

Farm!' She zoomed off.
'I'll do some skating
practice at the ice
rink,' Yasmin said.
'Could I use my
changer charm?'
'Yes.' Stella nodded.
Cassie watched
Yasmin concentrate on a
tiny mirror charm. With a
swirl of sparkles, Yasmin's
trainers became white
ice skates!
'See you!'
she cried, and
whooshed across the
Starry Sky.

Cassie hugged Stella. She knew that if she didn't find her bracelet she might never see her magical friend again.

'I'll come back to the pink star tonight with my bracelet,' Cassie promised. 'Then you'll be back to your sparkly, magical self! You'll see!'

As Cassie said goodbye, Stella's shadowy form was barely visible among the bright bobbing stars.

When Cassie flew through the open glass panel in her bedroom ceiling, she found

Alex sitting on her bed, with his white puppy, Comet, curled up beside Twinkle. Alex and Cassie had become best friends last summer when his family stayed at the Starwatcher Towers B & B. Now he lived in Astral-on-Sea, but he was staying with Cassie while his parents were away.

'Is Stella OK?' he asked.

'Not really,' said Cassie. 'She says I must swim in the gala if I'm to find my bracelet.'

'I wonder why. It doesn't seem very logical,' Alex said. He shrugged and got up. 'Shall I make your breakfast while you change?'

'Thanks!' said Cassie.

She put on shorts and a T-shirt over her

swimming costume, polished off a bowl
of cereal and grabbed her swimming bag.
They called goodbye to Cassie's parents and
headed down the hill towards the beach
with Comet.

The Swimming Gala Wish

'What's the swimming gala like?' asked Alex.

'There are races for different ages,' said Cassie, 'and a beginners' race, and funny ones with rubber ducks and hoops for little children. I'm in the Under-9 Freestyle. My friend Danny and I have practised all year.'

'You must be good,' said Alex.

Cassie grinned. 'Danny's *much* faster than me,' she said, 'because he practises harder. He's determined to win.'

At the beach, Alex took a red ball from his

pocket and threw it for Comet. 'Fetch it!' he cried.

Comet brought the ball back, his tail

wagging furiously. 'Good boy!' said Alex. He and Comet played while Cassie got ready for her event. She wondered why it was important for her to be in the race. Everything seemed normal. The sea was calm, holidaymakers explored the pier, people queued at the candyfloss kiosk and the beach was filling with spectators for the gala.

Cassie's friend Bert came by with his string of donkeys. 'No rides until after the gala,' he said.

'Why, will the cheering frighten them?' asked Cassie, patting Coco, her favourite.

Bert
chuckled.
'Not likely,'
he said.
'They're used
to yelling
children. No,
I'm not giving
rides because
I want to watch the
races!'

He wished Cassie luck and strolled
away.

The judges had taken up position by the
finish line, which was marked by a banner
stretched above the water between two
poles.

The twenty metres doggy-paddle got
under way.

Cassie was beginning to
feel jittery and, when
Danny arrived, she
thought he looked
as nervous as she
felt.

'Good luck, Cassie,'
he said, then grinned.
'Even though I really

wish I was fast enough to win!'

'Me too!' she laughed. 'Good luck!'

As Danny sat down next to Alex, Cassie drew a sharp breath. Danny had made a wish! Then she remembered. How could she grant wishes without her bracelet? What a shame – Danny had trained so hard that he deserved to win.

I couldn't control a race, anyway, she thought. *That would be unfair.*

Cassie heard a yell. Hannah and Yasmin were running towards her, followed by their parents.

Cassie introduced them to Danny. They already knew Alex, and Comet was excited to see them again.

The announcer's megaphone clicked.

The Swimming Gala Wish

'Can we have the Under-9 Freestyle contestants in the water, please?' the voice boomed.

'Time for your race,' Alex said.

'Wish me luck,' said Cassie.

As she joined the other competitors at the starting line, her tummy fluttered. She and Danny gave each other a thumbs-up.

33

The announcer said, 'On your marks . . .
Get set . . . Oh! A late contestant is joining
the race!'

Cassie turned. It was Donna Fox! Her
parents owned Flashley Manor, the poshest
hotel in Astral-on-Sea. They were helping
Donna out of her fluffy pink robe and glitzy
gold sandals.

As Donna waded
into the water for
the race, Cassie
thought how
Donna had
spent the last
two days
boasting
that she
would win.

Donna
looked at
her. 'I don't
know why
you're bothering,' she said, twirling
a pair of gold goggles studded with
crystals. 'I'll win.'

'You don't know that,' said Cassie. 'There are some amazing swimmers here. Danny's won a trophy.'

Donna flicked her long blonde ponytail. 'Trophy, pah!' she sneered. 'My swimming is far superior. My swimming is so good it's – like magic!'

Cassie was furious. *She reckons all she needs to win is the flashiest outfit*, she thought. *Well, she hasn't practised like Danny and me.*

The Swimming Gala Wish

The announcer's voice boomed. 'On your marks . . . Get set . . . GO!'

They were off!

3

Time Travel

Donna's boasting had put Cassie off and she began the race badly. Danny had a slow start too, but was soon just ahead of Cassie. Now she put everything into the race, kicking her legs and pulling herself through the water with all her strength.

Cassie glanced to her left and saw she was ahead of Donna. *Hah!* Cassie thought. *She was too busy showing off!*

Cassie ploughed on, then checked

again to see where the others were. Danny
was still in the lead, but what was Donna
doing?

Cassie saw her look towards the beach,
where Bert stood near the finish with
his donkeys. Donna yelled one word:
'RUN!'

Suddenly the donkeys scattered, braying.
'Hee-haw-hee-haw!'

When Coco dashed right into the
water, Cassie was so startled, she stopped
swimming for a moment. Danny did the
same, then they both struck out again
strongly, swimming for the line.

But Donna appeared to almost fly
through the water as she overtook Danny.
Cassie couldn't believe her eyes. How

could she swim so fast? Had she been
practising in secret?

Donna zoomed across the finish line.
Danny was second, then Cassie splashed
up in third place to hear Donna crowing,

'I've won! I told you I'd win!'

As Cassie got her breath back, she wondered how Donna had managed to make the donkeys scatter. The noise of the gala didn't bother them, and surely they didn't understand the word 'run'.

Then, as Donna spun round, punching her fist into the air, Cassie saw something that shocked her so much all she could do was stare, unable to utter a word.

The Swimming Gala Wish

There were sparkles
dancing around
Donna's ponytail!
Cassie knew those
sparkles well –
they were the
same ones that
surrounded her
bracelet whenever she used its magic.

Donna Fox had stolen the bracelet! As
Cassie looked closer, she could see it woven
into Donna's ponytail, hidden beneath a
glittery gold hair bobble.

*That's why Stella wanted me to swim in the
gala*, she thought.

Now Cassie knew how Donna had won
the race. She'd cheated. With the bracelet's

crescent-moon charm the donkeys had understood when she'd told them to run, and with the bird charm she had flown through the water.

The bracelet's magical powers should only be used to help others, not for yourself, Cassie thought angrily, *and certainly not to cheat!*

The most awful thing is that because Donna stole my bracelet, Stella is disappearing! Cassie clenched her fists. She had to get the bracelet

back – before it was too late.

She was splashing her way towards
Donna when suddenly everything
around her went still. The swimmers, the
spectators, even the waves stopped moving.
It was as if someone had pressed 'pause',
and brought time to a halt.

Cassie thought at first that Donna had
used her butterfly charm to stop time. But
Donna, too, was completely still. What was
happening?

She looked towards the crowd,
standing like statues on the beach, and
saw Alex, frozen in the act of picking
up Comet. But Yasmin was waving, and
Hannah was jangling her bracelet and
pointing at it!

Just then, sparkles swirled around Cassie and something even weirder happened.

Time started moving backwards.

4
Lucky Stars Together

Cassie found herself swimming in reverse! Her arms went the wrong way and instead of getting closer the finish line got further away with each stroke.

Then she ran backwards across the sand until she was talking to Alex, just as she had before the race. But her words were back to front!

'Luck me wish,' Cassie said.

'Race your for time,' he replied.

Alex didn't seem to notice anything odd,
but Cassie realized what was happening.
This was Lucky Stars magic! Hannah and
Yasmin were helping her out, just as they'd
promised.

Cassie spoke to Danny and Bert,
and even stroked Coco the donkey –
backwards. Next she was putting on her
T-shirt and shorts.

'Boy good!' cried Alex as Comet picked
up his ball and ran in reverse across the
sand. Next thing, the ball was flying back
through the air into Alex's hand.

'It fetch!' he cried.

Suddenly, everything stopped, just for
a split second. Then time moved again –
forward now.

48

The Swimming Gala Wish

'Alex, listen!' said Cassie. 'We've gone back in time, and—'

'Gone back in time? Wow! So time travel *is* possible,' he breathed. 'Scientists have tried, and no one's ever achieved it — but *I* have!'

'Hannah's got a rewind charm,' Cassie told him. 'The race has already happened and Donna won. She stole my bracelet and she cheated!'

For a moment, Alex was speechless. 'I knew she was mean, but I didn't think she'd do a thing like that!' he said at last.

'Do you think Hannah and Yasmin realized she had it? Perhaps they made time rewind so you could get it back before the race.'

'You're right!' said Cassie, looking around. 'Where *are* Hannah and Yasmin?'

'Use your charm,' said Alex. 'It can take you to other Lucky Stars.'

'Of course!' said Cassie, taking the silver star from her pocket. She clutched Alex's arm. 'Hold Comet's paw,' she said, 'and get ready for star travel.'

Sand, sunbathers and playing children swirled around them. Cassie felt as if she was in a whirling sea of stars.

The sparkles faded. They were standing

by the sweeping front steps of Flashley
Manor Hotel – Donna's home. Waiting for
them were Hannah and Yasmin!

Hannah grinned. 'My rewind charm worked then!' she said, showing them a tiny silver clock on her bracelet. 'It makes time go backwards.'

'Amazing,' said Alex, peering at it. 'Until today I didn't think time travel was scientifically possible.'

'It's magic, not science,' said Cassie. 'We must get my Lucky Star bracelet back before the gala starts, or Stella will . . .' She swallowed. 'She'll disappear.'

Yasmin squeezed Cassie's shoulder. 'How can we get into the hotel without someone asking what we're up to?' she asked.

Alex pointed to a nearby sign. It said:

FLASHLEY MANOR'S LUXURIOUS
POOL IS OPEN TO ALL DURING
GALA WEEK

NO SHOUTING ❖ NO RUNNING
NO DIVE-BOMBING ❖ NO PUSHING

MEMBERSHIP AVAILABLE

'Great!' said Yasmin. 'We'll pretend
we've come to swim.' She selected her
silver mirror charm. 'I use this to change
outfits and disguise myself when I'm
granting wishes,' she said. 'Everyone hold
hands!'

They formed a ring. Instantly,

shimmering sparkles wove over and
between them.

'Wow!' said Cassie, looking down at
her floaty orange tunic over a gorgeous
sunshine-yellow swimsuit. Yasmin's outfit
was covered in sea-green swirls, and
Hannah's was the same rose pink as her
plaited leather necklace.

'Donna mustn't see your bracelets,'
Cassie warned.

'No problem for my transformer charm!'

said Hannah, taking
Yasmin's hand.
Sparkles danced
around their
wrists, and the
bracelets vanished! In

their place were underwater watches.

They approached the pool and saw
Donna on a sunlounger. She wore a
crimson silk tunic over her swimsuit
and huge sunglasses with gold frames
that glittered in the sunlight. She held
an enormous glass of juice with whole
strawberries floating in it. Topping it was a
little red paper umbrella.

Donna took a long drink from the twisty
straw, turned to put the glass down and saw
the visitors.

She groaned. 'Not you two again,' she
said to Cassie and Alex. 'What a cheek,
bringing your friends in. *And* that dog.' She
tugged her sleeve down. 'I can't bear it when
Mummy and Daddy let just *anybody* in.'

Cassie knew what Donna's sleeve was hiding. 'I've lost my charm bracelet,' she said. 'Have you seen it?'

Donna tugged her sleeve again. 'No. Why would I have?'

56

As Cassie walked past with the others, she whispered, 'I gave her a chance to give it back but she didn't. So we'll have to make her take it off.'

Alex nodded. 'You're right,' he said quietly. 'But how?'

'I don't know,' said Cassie, 'but I have to get it back – for Stella's sake.'

5
Cheat!

The girls slid into the pool while Alex told
Comet, 'Stay!' The puppy sat by the side of
the water.

'He's getting really obedient,' Alex said,
joining Cassie in the pool. 'He can sit,
fetch and stay.' He frowned gloomily. 'If
I'd taught him "on guard", your bracelet
wouldn't have been stolen.'

Cassie smiled. 'Alex, it wasn't your
fault.'

Hannah swam over. 'Laugh and have fun,' she said, 'then Donna won't realize we're plotting.'

Cassie splashed about and Yasmin giggled loudly.

Alex ducked under the water and came up spluttering. 'That's interesting. When the pool's churned up by people splashing, it's hard to see underwater. Probably something to do with light bending—'

'Alex, that's it!' Cassie interrupted. 'Let's get Donna to swim underwater. If it's hard to see, maybe I could get close and slide the bracelet off her wrist. She'll just think someone bumped into her!'

'It could work,' Alex said. 'And I

know how to get Donna in the pool! My observations show that she likes to win, right?'

Cassie nodded.

'Then let's hold an underwater race!' said Alex.

'Brilliant!' Cassie said. 'Donna can't resist a chance to show off.'

They climbed out and stood at the edge of the pool as if they were about to dive in.

'Is everybody ready?' Yasmin called, louder than necessary.

They all yelled, 'Yes!' and Cassie whispered, 'Is Donna looking?'

'Yes,' Hannah hissed. 'She's coming over.'

'Ready?' called Yasmin.

They stretched out their arms and bent forward, as if they were about to plunge into the water. Suddenly they heard Donna's voice.

'You lot! What are you doing?'

Cassie looked up. 'It's a race,' she said. 'Whoever swims the furthest underwater without taking a breath wins.'

'I'll win,' said Hannah, grinning.

'No, I will,' said Yasmin.

'Rubbish!' laughed Alex. 'Cassie or I will win easily.'

Donna smirked. 'I could beat the lot of you!'

'OK,' Cassie said. 'Prove it.'

Donna hesitated.

Cassie held her breath. Would she fall for it?

'Right,' said Donna, pulling off her tunic. 'Here I come, losers!'

Cassie noticed that Donna kept one hand behind her back as she lined up next to

them by the pool, hiding the bracelet.

'Ready?' Yasmin yelled when everyone
was lined up. '*Go!*'

They dived underwater. Cassie
immediately looked to her left where
Donna should be, but no one was there.
She couldn't swim underwater that fast,
could she?

Cassie pushed up to the surface.
Donna was already at the far end of
the pool, looking pleased with herself.
Once Hannah, Yasmin and Alex had
spluttered to the surface halfway down
the pool, Donna announced, 'I swam
underwater further than any of you.
I'm the winner!'

'Congratulations,' everyone said as
Donna climbed out. She grabbed a
towel from a sunlounger to cover the
bracelet.

Cassie could see the others were surprised
that Donna had swum so fast. She was
annoyed she'd missed her chance to get
near her.

Then Alex pulled Cassie close,

whispering, 'She never went underwater at all. Her hair's dry, and – look – there's even a leaf caught in it from up in that tree.'

Cassie gasped. 'She used my bracelet to win! First she used my cupcake charm to make herself invisible, then the bird charm to help her fly to the other end! Ooh, the . . . the . . .'

'Cheat!' said Hannah and Yasmin together.

Cassie lay back and floated, looking at the clouds. Stella was somewhere up there in the Starry Sky. *I must get that bracelet*, she thought. Aloud, she muttered, 'How do you trick someone as sneaky as Donna?'

Yasmin checked her watch. 'I don't know,' she said, 'but we'd better hurry!

The Swimming Gala Wish

It'll soon be time for the swimming gala to begin. If we're not careful, we'll be late!'

6
Donna Shows Off

The friends hid behind a hedge and
Yasmin used her mirror charm to dress
them, then they collected Comet from the
poolside.

Mrs Fox was bringing a fresh drink for
Donna. 'Hello, Cassie!' she called, then
said, 'Donna, darling, why not take your
little friends to your bedroom?'

Donna stood, arms folded, and snapped,
'What for?'

'To show them all your lovely presents,' Mrs Fox continued.

Donna smirked. 'Oh yeah,' she said.

'Everyone loves my darling girl,' said Mrs Fox. 'She's been given so many lovely things lately. Who gave you all the presents, my pet?'

'Guests, mainly,' Donna said airily. 'To thank me for being kind and helpful. Come on, you lot.' She led them indoors, ignoring a guest who asked where the dining room was.

'Can't imagine anyone giving *her* a present,' whispered Yasmin. 'She's so rude.'

They followed Donna up a grand staircase and along a thickly carpeted

corridor to a door
marked 'Private'.

Comet put his
nose to the bottom
of the door and
sniffed.

'Pick that animal
up,' Donna said. 'I
don't want dog fur
all over my things.'

Alex swept Comet into his arms and they
went in.

Donna's bedroom was enormous, with
windows overlooking the sea. A vast
television was mounted on one wall, beside
a shelf unit stacked with DVDs, and a
huge walk-in wardrobe full of clothes. On

the floor were expensive-looking bags, toys, books, shoes, games, two laptops and another TV.

With all this stuff, it looks like Donna sits up

here all alone, Cassie thought. For a moment, Cassie felt sorry for her. Donna flung open a cupboard door to show off her jewellery stands and vast collection of hair accessories.

'I've got seventeen pairs of jeans,' Donna boasted, totally engrossed in the contents of the cupboard, 'two karaoke machines, three games consoles, two tablets . . .'

Cassie nudged Alex. 'This is so weird. How come she's suddenly been given all this stuff without Mrs Fox even knowing who it's from? Did it all appear out of nowhere?' she whispered.

Alex stared at her, and she could tell that he had been thinking the same thing. 'It's magic, isn't it?' she gasped. 'Donna's

used my flower charm to give herself these presents!'

'You're right,' he said. 'How greedy is she?'

Cassie only had to look around to see how greedy Donna was. That gave her an idea. *But would it work . . . ?* she thought.

Donna was showing off her three smartphones to Hannah and Yasmin, so Cassie whispered, 'Alex, can you keep Donna busy while I talk to the others?'

He nodded. Then he said loudly, 'Donna, is your television 3D?'

'Of course it is. And it's got surround sound,' she replied grandly. 'I'll show you.' She picked up a remote and the TV blared into life.

While Donna flicked through the channels, Cassie whispered to Hannah and Yasmin, 'Donna's been using my magic charm bracelet to get all this stuff.'

'Of course!' said Hannah.

Yasmin frowned. 'Rude *and* greedy.'

'Let's tempt her with something that seems even better than my bracelet,' said Cassie.

'Like what?' said Yasmin, but Hannah had an idea.

'My changer charm will do the trick,' she said. She unclasped the rose-pink leather necklace from her neck, and fastened it round Cassie's.

Hannah's changer charm had a cute monkey face on one side and an apple

on the other. As it spun, it flickered . . .
Monkey, apple, monkey, apple . . .

Sparkles streamed
from the charm to the
pink necklace and
Cassie felt it grow
heavier. She looked
down and saw that
it had become a
chunky chain
laden with silver charms – far more than on
her bracelet.

'Wow! There are so many charms!' said
Yasmin. 'Look at the ballerina – oh, and
that cute little panda . . .'

Hannah grinned. 'Imagine the powers
they'd have if they were real.'

'Let's hope Donna thinks the same,' Cassie muttered.

'I've allowed a few sparkles to dance round it,' whispered Hannah. 'They look magical, but they're not.'

'Let's hope they're enough to fool Donna!' Cassie said as Donna snapped off the TV. 'We're about to find out!'

7
A Gift for Donna

Alex turned round from the TV. The three girls laughed. He was wearing 3D glasses, instead of his own.

Donna snatched them off. 'Don't be silly,' she said. Then she spotted Cassie's necklace. 'Where did that come from?'

Cassie flicked a charm with her finger. 'This?

I've worn it all day,' she said. 'Didn't you notice? Maybe it's invisible in some lights. Like magic!'

Donna looked suspicious. 'Where did you get it?'

Cassie turned to leave. 'It was to replace the bracelet that I lost. They were from the same person.' She jingled the charms. 'The necklace is loads better!'

Donna grabbed Cassie's arm, pulled her round and stared at the necklace.

Cassie thought, *I've never seen anyone look so greedy*.

'Let me try it on,' said Donna.

Cassie pretended to hesitate.

'Go on,' Donna snapped. 'What are you afraid of?'

Cassie removed the necklace. Donna snatched it and clasped it round her own neck.

'It suits you,' said Cassie. 'Look, keep it if you want – as a sort of thank-you for letting us use your pool.'

Donna peered warily at Cassie. 'If this necklace is so great,' she said, 'why would you give it away?'

Cassie leaned forward and whispered,
'Can you keep a secret?'

'Yes,' said Donna. 'What?'

In the mirror, Cassie saw the others
admiring the presents and guessed they
were listening.

'*What?*' Donna demanded.

'It's a magical necklace,' said Cassie. 'See
the sparkles?'

Donna's eyes were enormous.

'The problem is,' Cassie explained,
'I've had some awful muddles with it. I
keep forgetting which charm does what.
Then I get loads of stuff I don't want, and
sometimes I can't stop it. That makes my
parents mad.'

Donna looked excited. 'Lots of charms,'

82

she muttered. 'I'd remember
them. Better than this
old bracelet . . . Much
better . . .'

Alex wandered
over. 'Cassie's right,'
he said. 'Starwatcher
Towers is so crammed
with stuff there's hardly
any room for guests. What with the ponies
in the garden . . .'

'Ponies?' cried Donna.

Cassie gave a great sigh. 'At this rate,
we'll soon have to move,' she said. 'And
where would Dad find another observatory?
You'd do us a favour if you took the
necklace.'

Donna jumped up and down, screeching with excitement. 'Oooh! I'm going to have SO many presents!' She pulled the bracelet off and flung it across the room. 'Here! I won't need *that* any more!'

Cassie watched as her bracelet landed on the bed. She wanted to run over and scoop it up, but she knew that would make Donna suspicious. She edged towards it while Donna was busy rubbing the charms on the necklace.

'Come on!' Donna snapped, rubbing furiously. 'How do you make it work?' She shook the charms. 'Come *on*! Oh, this is useless.' She turned, saw Cassie heading for the bracelet and shrieked in fury. 'You tricked me!'

Cassie was three steps away from the bed. She glared at Donna. 'Yes, I tricked you,' she said, 'but you stole my bracelet! Those charms are for helping people – not to get things for yourself.'

Donna gave a squeal. 'You've got everything, haven't you? A magic bracelet – lots of friends. It's not fair!'

Yasmin stepped between them. 'Donna, we're friends with Cassie because she's kind and helpful and fun. If you were like that, we'd be your friends too.'

'Pah!' Donna shoved Yasmin and Cassie aside, and they all fell on the floor. She dived for the bed, but Alex was quicker. 'Fetch!' he told Comet, and pointed to the bracelet.

The puppy leaped on the bed and

grabbed the bracelet. He and Alex darted from the room followed by Hannah, Yasmin and Cassie.

Donna tore after them, howling with rage.

The Swimming Gala Wish

They ran downstairs, past Mrs Fox and
out of the front door, with Donna shrieking
after them, 'You wait, Cassie Cafferty!'

'Darling!' called Mrs Fox. 'What's wrong?
Ooh, who gave you that lovely necklace?'

Cassie didn't hear Donna's reply.

Once they were safely away, Cassie
slipped her bracelet back on. Instantly,
sparkles streamed around her and she felt
a great feeling of happiness and joy well
up inside. Tonight she would go to the
pink star and show Stella that she'd got her
bracelet back, and Stella would be back to
her bright, sparkly, magical self.

'Cassie, your race is about to start!' said
Yasmin, checking her watch. 'Hurry!'

★

The spectators were cheering the swimmers on.

'Go, Cassie!'

'Dan-*nee*! Dan-*nee*!'

Cassie ploughed through the water. Donna hadn't turned up, so nothing could spoil the race. She put on a final spurt, but Danny had the lead and he finished first.

'You won!' Cassie cried. 'Well done, Danny!'

She turned back to shore, feeling happy. Danny had made a wish to win the race. By stopping Donna's cheating, Cassie made it come true. That was the work of a Lucky Star.

On the beach she was greeted by cheers

from Hannah, Yasmin, their parents and
Alex.

Cassie hugged her friends. 'Thank you,'
she said. 'I would never have got my
bracelet back without you. Together we've
saved Stella!'

'*Yup!*' Comet barked.

Cassie scooped him up. 'You were the
best help of all!' She laughed.

That night, Cassie flew across the Starry
Sky to the pink star.

'Stella!' she breathed. Her friend was just
the faintest outline now, barely visible.

She touched Stella's arm. 'Look,' she said
softly, holding out her wrist.

When Stella saw the shining bracelet, she

cried out in delight. 'You found it! Well done, Cassie.'

She took Cassie's hands and whirled her around in a mist of sparkles. When they let go of each other, Cassie could see Stella clearly again. Her silvery clothes and sparkling crown gleamed, and her

90

wand showered tiny, brilliant stars into the darkness.

'Your powers are back!' Cassie cried.

'Thanks to you. You're a very special Lucky Star, Cassie,' Stella said. 'You'll have many more magical adventures to come!' She took Cassie's hand. 'Let's fly!'

As they soared joyfully together across the Starry Sky, Cassie thought, *I couldn't be happier. It's wonderful to be a Lucky Star!*

Cassie's Things to Make and Do!

Join in the Lucky Stars fun!

Head It Or Catch It

This can be played in the swimming pool or in the shallow water at the beach.

★ Everyone should stand in a circle in the water with one person in the middle.

★ The person in the middle should have a ball to throw to the players round the circle.

★ As they throw the ball they should shout either 'head it' or 'catch it', and the player they aim it at needs to react quickly to follow the command.

★ Anyone who gets their action wrong has to leave the pool or water.

★ The winner is the person left in the water at the end.

Synchronized Swimmers

Have a look at these two pictures.

Can you spot four differences between them?

Hold a Mini Swimming Gala

★ Invite all your friends to a swimming party, either at the beach or at your local swimming pool.

★ During the day you can hold different races – try front crawl, backstroke, breaststroke and freestyle.

⭐ Make sure you bring along prizes for the winners!

Swimming Wordsearch

Can you find all the words below in the grid opposite?

FRONT CRAWL
BACKSTROKE
POOL
BELLYFLOP
DIVE
FREESTYLE

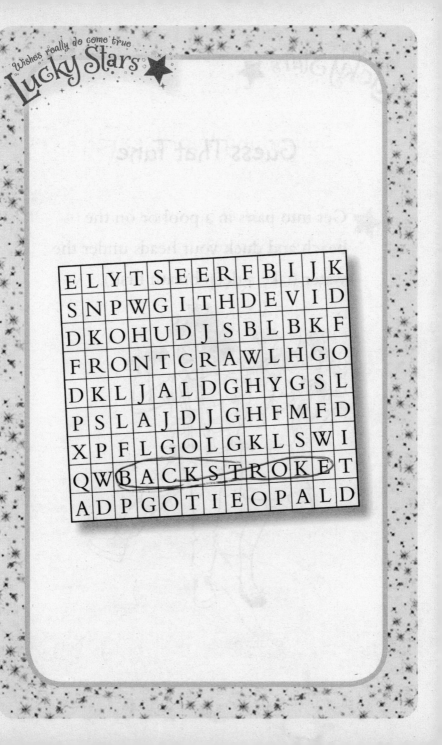

E	L	Y	T	S	E	E	R	F	B	I	J	K
S	N	P	W	G	I	T	H	D	E	V	I	D
D	K	O	H	U	D	J	S	B	L	B	K	F
F	R	O	N	T	C	R	A	W	L	H	G	O
D	K	L	J	A	L	D	G	H	Y	G	S	L
P	S	L	A	J	D	J	G	H	F	M	F	D
X	P	F	L	G	O	L	G	K	L	S	W	I
Q	W	B	A	C	K	S	T	R	O	K	E	T
A	D	P	G	O	T	I	E	O	P	A	L	D

Guess That Tune

★ Get into pairs in a pool or on the beach and duck your heads under the water (take a deep breath first!).

One person
should hum a
tune for five
seconds, and the
other one has to
guess what it is.

 Take it in turns to hum – the
person who guesses the most tunes
correctly is the winner!

Answers

Don't look unless
you're really stuck!

Synchronized Swimmers

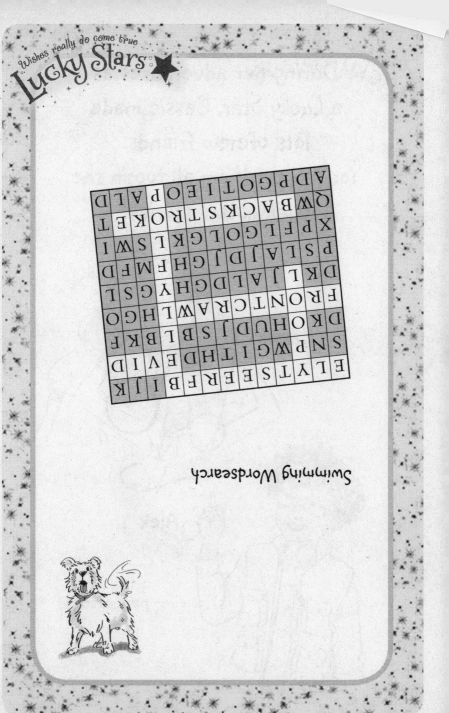

Swimming Wordsearch

During her adventures as
a Lucky Star, Cassie made
lots of new friends.
You'll meet them all too in the
Lucky Stars stories!

Cassie

Alex

Comet

Twinkle

Stella

Hannah

Kate

Donna

Cassie's mum

Cassie's dad

The Best Friend Wish

Phoebe Bright

With a whizz, fizz
and pop, magical Stella
Starkeeper appears and tells
Cassie she will be a Lucky Star –
someone who can grant wishes.
Could Alex, her new friend,
have a secret wish?

The Perfect Pony Wish

Phoebe Bright

Sunbeam the pony has
run away! Cassie must help
a little girl's wish come true and
find him before the showjumping
competition begins. Will
Sunbeam be the perfect pony?

Wishes really do come true

Lucky Stars

The Pop Singer Wish

Phoebe Bright

Pop sensation
Jacey Day is performing
in Astral-on-Sea, but her
backing singers are ill! Jacey
wishes someone could fix things . . .
Cassie must find a way for
the show to go on!

Wishes really do come true... Lucky Stars

Explore the magical world of Lucky Stars!

For fun things to make and do – as well as games and quizzes – go to:

www.luckystarsbooks.co.uk

Wishes really do come true
Lucky Stars

Cassie is training to become a Lucky Star –
someone who can make wishes come true!
Follow her on more exciting adventures as
she meets new friends in need of help.

www.luckystarsbooks.co.uk